FOR FRED. DUFFELL
M.W.

my
great
Granpa

FOR MOM
D.M.

Published in 1990 by G.P. Putnam's Sons, a division of The Putnam
& Grosset Group, 200 Madison Avenue, New York, NY 10016.
Originally published in Great Britain by Walker Books Ltd.
Printed by South China Printing Co., Hong Kong
Library of Congress Cataloging-in-Publication Data
Waddell, Martin.
My great grandpa.
Summary: A girl describes her special times with her
great-grandfather, who may be slow and weak but still
travels to places in his mind where no one else can go.
[1. Grandfathers—Fiction. 2. Old age—Fiction]
I. Mansell, Dom, ill. II. Title.
PZ7.W1137My 1990   [E]   89-10471
ISBN O-399-22155-7

1 3 5 7 9 10 8 6 4 2

First American Edition

My Great Grandpa

Written by

Martin Waddell

Illustrated by

Dom Mansell

G.P. Putnam's Sons
New York

My Great Grandpa is slow.
His eyes are weak and
his legs don't go.
But he knows things that
no one else knows,
things he tells me about
when we go out.

Sometimes we go when my
Granny doesn't know.
He calls me his bus driver.
I call him my baby.
He makes bussy noises and
I push his chair.
People stare,
but we don't care!

My Great Grandpa knows
all about our town,
who lived where and
when and how.
But he can't remember who
lives here *now*.
So I have to tell him.
He says I'm as smart as a button,
but a button isn't much.

Our favorite place is his old house at the
bend at the end of the lane.
We go there again and again and
again and again and again and again.
We call it our house.

My Great Grandpa says it was his house
when Granny was like me, his little mouse.
But I'm not a mouse,
I'm a LION!

He says my Great Granny had eyes like mine
and they'd shine.
Then he sits for a while and starts to smile
and I think it's nice
because he loves her
. . . still.

My Great Grandpa knows where the berries are,
but it's too far.
We don't go picking berries.
We get them in Ted's shop instead.
Great Grandpa says berries
are bad for his burps,
but he eats so many
you'd think he would burst,
almost as many as me.

My Great Grandpa says I'm his special girl,
like my Granny was when she was young,
and my Mom and then me.
He says we are peas in a pod.
I say I'm a runner bean!
And then he says, "Let's go to the swings."

My Great Grandpa doesn't swing or do *anything*.
He sits and he nods and he smiles.
And he thinks of the things that he knows
that no one else knows.
He calls himself "Crow on the Shelf."
He's the nicest old crow that I know,
and I tell him so.

The sun makes Great Grandpa hot and grumpy.
So we go home.
And he goes to bed to rest his old head.

And I sit with my Granny on the grass in the sun.
She says, "It's sad to be like
Great Grandpa is now!"

But I know it's NOT!
For my Great Grandpa knows things
that no one else knows.
In his mind he goes places
that no one else goes.
He's got me, he's got Granny
and my Mom,
and we love him a lot . . .

but he shouldn't go out
when it's hot!